a minedition book
published by Penguin Young Readers Group

First published in German under the title NORi, Gute Nacht!
Text copyright © 2007 Brigitte Weninger
Illustrations copyright © 2007 by Yusuke Yonezu
Coproduction with Michael Neugebauer Publishing Ltd., Hong Kong
Rights arranged with "minedition" Rights and Licensing AG, Zurich, Switzerland
Published simultaneously in Canada
Manufactured in Hong Kong by Wide World Ltd.
Typesetting in Arial Rounded
Color separation by Fotoriproduzione Beverari, Verona, Italy

Library of Congress Cataloging-in-Publication Data available upon request.
ISBN 978-0-698-40065-8
10 9 8 7 6 5 4 3 2 1
First Impression

Good Night, NORi

Brigitte Weninger
Pictures by
Yusuke Yonezu

Translated by Kathryn Bishop

min·dition

It was time to go to bed.
The stars were already twinkling in the sky.
Nori brushed his teeth
and slid down under the covers.

But Norr couldn't get to sleep.
He tossed and turned
and then he tossed some more, but it didn't help!
"I wonder what my friends are doing?" he thought.

Outside in the moonlight it was peaceful.
Lotti Lamb was sleeping in the meadow
on a soft bed of grass.
"Baaa..."said Lotti sleepily.
"Nori, it's late, what are you doing up?"
"I can't sleep!" said Nori.

"Oh, my," said Lotti. "Maybe your pillow is too hard.
Would you like to try one like mine?"
Nori nodded, so Lotti filled a bag with sweet
dry grass from the meadow.
"Now your bed will smell like summer," said Lotti.
"Oh, thank you, Lotti," said Nori. "Good night."
"Good night, Nori."

Nori saw Henrietta Hen in the henhouse.
"Peep, peep, peep," said Henrietta softly.
"Nori, it's late, what are you doing out of bed?"
"I can't sleep," whispered Nori.
"Can I play with One, Two and Three
   for a little while?"

"At this time of night?" said Henrietta. "I'm afraid not.
Night-time is growing time for children, you know.
But here, maybe a dream feather will help.
Sweet dreams, Nori!"
"Thank you," said Nori. "Good night."

By the big tree Nori found Ella Elephant.
"Too-too-too," tooted Ella, very surprised.
"Nori, it's late, you should be asleep!"
"I can't sleep," said Nori.
"Why not?" asked Ella.

"Because I'm...I'm... all by myself," stuttered Nori.
"I see," said Ella. "Take the little one with you.
I'm much too big for your bed but
he can stay with you and protect you! Good night!"
"Good night, Ella, and thank you!" said Nori.

Petey Pig was cozy, wallowing in his muddy bed.
"Oink, oink, Nori, it's late, you should be in bed!" he said.
"I can't sleep," said Nori.
"Hmm," thought Petey.
"Then someone should tell you a bedtime story!"

"But everybody's sleeping," said Nori.
"All you need to do is open the window," said Petey.
"Mr. Moon is there and the stars will certainly tell you something wonderful. They're always there if you need them. Sleep well, Nori!"
"Thank you, Petey. Good night!"

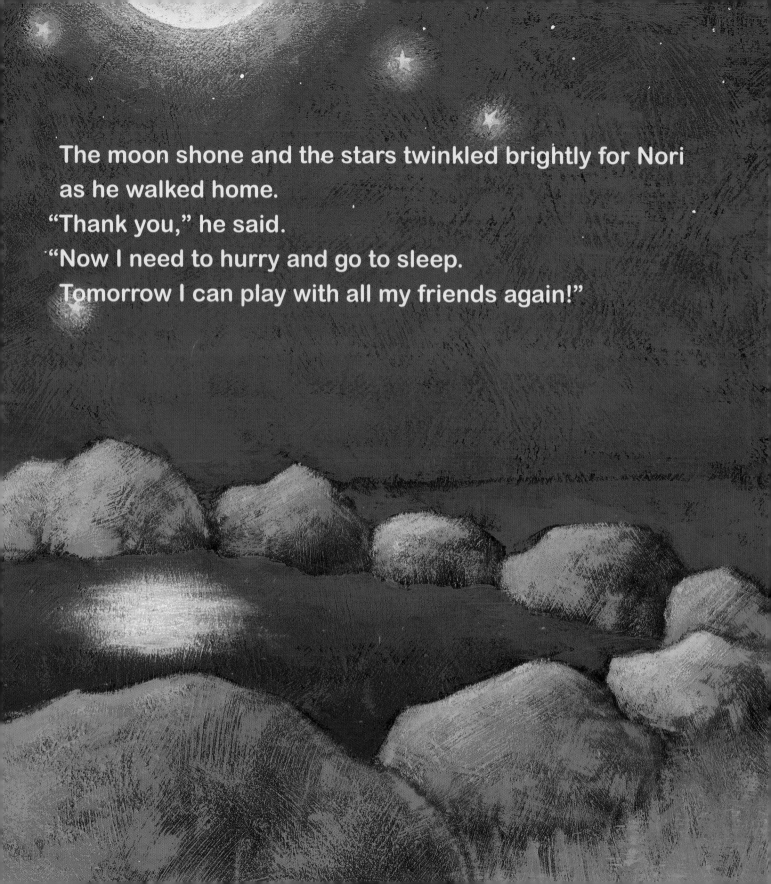

The moon shone and the stars twinkled brightly for Nori
as he walked home.
"Thank you," he said.
"Now I need to hurry and go to sleep.
Tomorrow I can play with all my friends again!"

"Good Night, Nori!"